W9-ASD-238

William and the Good Old Days

by Eloise Greenfield

illustrated by Jan Spivey Gilchrist

HarperCollins*Publishers*

William and the Good Old Days

Text copyright © 1993 by Eloise Greenfield

Illustrations copyright © 1993 by Jan Spivey Gilchrist

Printed in Mexico. All rights reserved.

Library of Congress Cataloging-in-Publication Data

Greenfield, Eloise.

William and the good old days / by Eloise Greenfield ;
illustrated by Jan Spivey Gilchrist.

p.   cm.

Summary: A little boy remembers his grandmother before she
became ill, and during her long recovery he tries to imagine how
things will be when she gets better.

ISBN 0-06-021093-1. — ISBN 0-06-021094-X (lib. bdg.)

[1. Grandmothers—Fiction. 2. Afro-Americans—Fiction.]
I. Gilchrist, Jan Spivey, ill.   II. Title.

PZ7.G845Wi 1993   91-47030

[E]—dc20   CIP

                                                                  AC

4 5 6 7 8 9 10 ❖

Here I go again, thinking about that fly and getting mad.

Yeah, I'm mad. That's because I *still* think it was that big, ugly fly that made my grandma sick. Mommy and Daddy say it wasn't, but I remember what happened that day.

I was sitting on this tall stool in Grandma's restaurant, eating my good dinner. Granddaddy and Mr. Frank were sitting on the other stools, and Miss Betty and Miss Lucille were sitting in the big chairs, and Grandma was standing at the stove, stirring the bean soup. Everybody was laughing and having a good old time.

Then, all of a sudden, I saw this fly, zooming around, zooming around, trying to get in everybody's food.

I said, "Grandma! There's a fly in here!"

Grandma said, "Oh, no!" Then she slammed the lid on the pot of soup, and she grabbed the box of shiny paper off the shelf and covered up the hot rolls. She said, "William, bring me that swatter!"

I got the swatter, and Grandma knocked the fly on the floor, and she hit him about a hundred times. And that was the end of that fly.

But right after that, about a week or a day after that fly upset my grandma, she got real sick and had to go to the hospital, and she stayed a long time.

And even though she's back at her house now, she's still sick, and her eyes can't see anymore.

But I don't like to think about that. I like to think about Grandma the way she used to be, back in the good old days, last year when I was little.

When I close my eyes, I can see that Grandma. I can see her hugging people, big people and children, too, and making them happy. And everybody calling her "Mama" even if she wasn't their mama. And if somebody who didn't know her came in the restaurant and didn't treat her nice, her friends looking at them funny and saying, "I *know* you not talking to *Mama* like that."

That's why Grandma named her restaurant "Mama's Kitchen," and every day the same people used to come there to eat their dinner. Sometimes they would help Grandma work. They'd say, "Mama, let me wash those collard greens for you." Or they'd clean the crumbs off the counter. And Miss Betty washed the dishes every day, just because she wanted to.

Mommy used to take me to the restaurant all the time, back in the good old days, and that was my favorite place to be. As soon as I got there, Grandma would say, "Well, here's my boy. You want some juice, William?"

I'd say, "Uh-huh. I'm *real* thirsty, Grandma."

Grandma would take me to the refrigerator, and I'd pick out *any* kind of juice I wanted. And after I drank it, I'd wash my hands and go help Grandma fold the napkins. When we finished, I'd lean over a little bit and hold my stomach.

"Grandma," I'd say, "I'm real hungry after all that work."

So Grandma would fix me a big plate of food. A piece of turkey wing and dressing and sweet potatoes and greens from her garden and yellow cornbread with just enough butter. And it was *so-o-o-o* good.

Every Saturday, Grandma used to cook chicken in the barbecue grill out in front of her restaurant. A whole lot of people would come and stand around and watch, and talk to each other, and talk to me, and make me laugh. I'd walk around and visit everybody, and when I got to Mr. Dennis, he always acted like he didn't even see me. So I'd tap him on his hand.

He'd frown and look up at the sky and say, "Uh-oh, think I felt a drop of rain."

I'd tap him again and say, "That doesn't feel like rain, Mr. Dennis."

He'd say, "William! Thank goodness it's you! Thought all our good chicken was going to be floating down Seventy-fifth Street."

I sure didn't want that to happen, because after Grandma finished cooking, we were all going inside to eat, and all those happy *people*-sounds would make my food taste extra, extra good.

Yeah, that was back in the good old days. But now, somebody else has Grandma's restaurant, and it's not named "Mama's Kitchen," and I don't go there anymore.

Everything is different, now that Grandma's sick. And even though I know it wasn't *really* the fly that did it, when I want to be mad about it and there's nobody to be mad at, I get mad at that fly, and then I feel better.

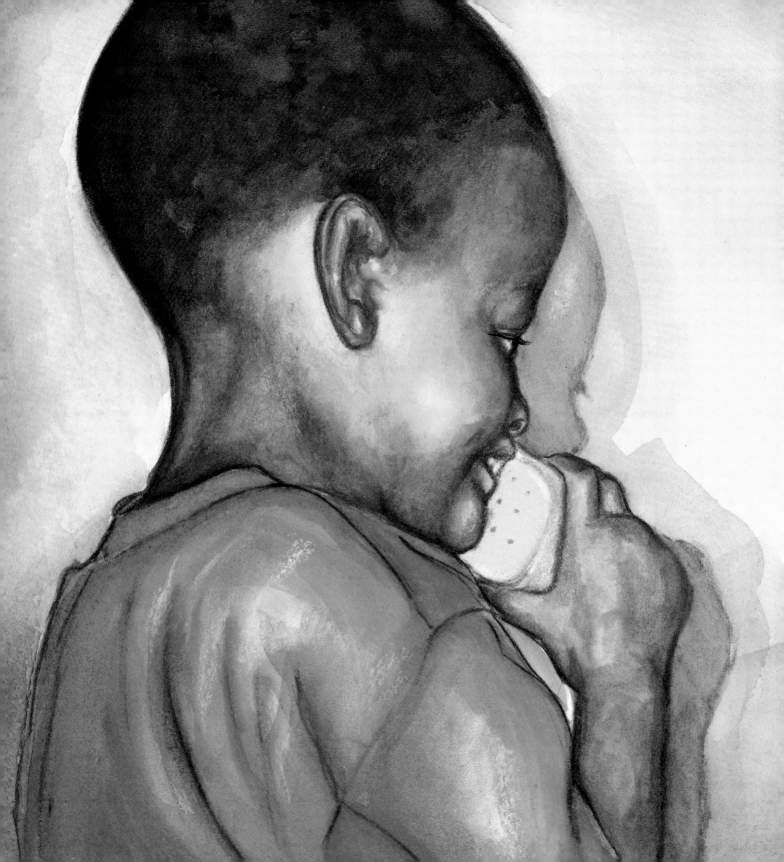

I want my grandma to feel better, too. So every day, I try to think of a whole lot of things to make her laugh. And then I call her up.

One day, when she answered the phone, I talked in my low voice. I said, "Hello, this is William's daddy."

Grandma said, "This ain't William?"

I said, "No, but hold on a minute, and I'll go get William for you." Then I talked in my real voice. I said, "That was me, Grandma! I was just fooling."

She said I really fooled her. It made her laugh, and she sounded a little bit like she used to.

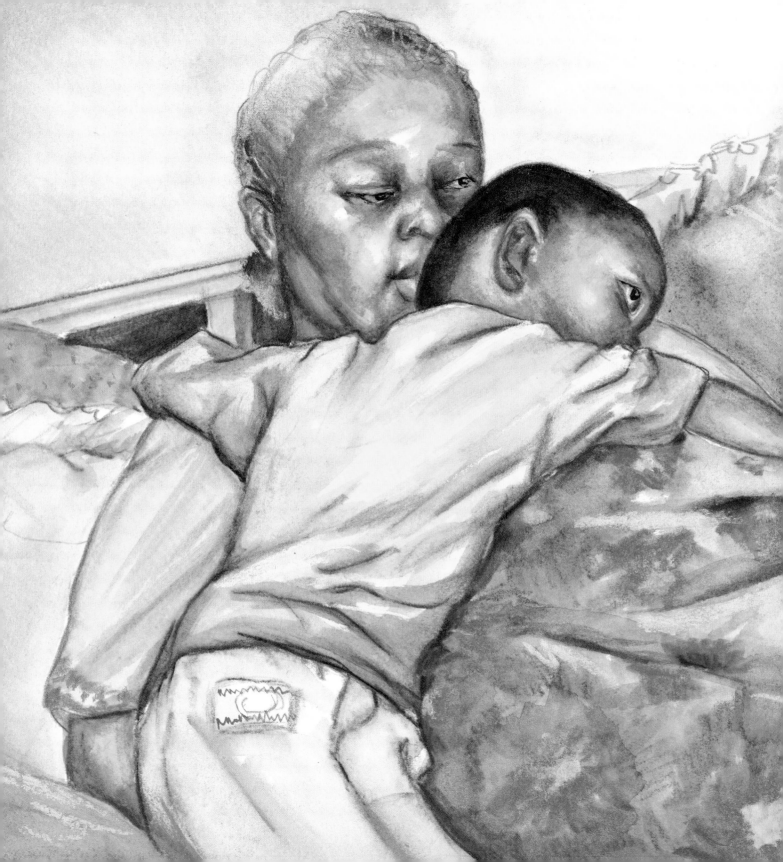

But yesterday, when Mommy and Daddy took me to her house, her face looked real tired, so I kissed it softly and I hugged her, but not too tight. Then I sat down beside her and we talked for a long time.

"I want you to be all the way well again," I said.

Grandma said that when she starts feeling better and the doctor says she can go out for a little while, she's going to come to my house and help me plant my garden. When I close my eyes, I can see just how it's going to be.

It will be spring, and the sun's going to be shining just right, not too hot, so Grandma can feel the pretty day on her arms. And I'm going to help Daddy bring our big, soft chair outside and put it beside the porch for her to sit in. And even though she can't see, she'll tell me just what to do.

I'll say, "Grandma, I have red flowers and blue flowers and yellow flowers and purple flowers."

And she'll say, "William, you know, I think the yellow would look real nice next to the red, and I think you want to put the blue next to the purple." And I'll plant everything just the way she tells me to.

Then we'll go inside the house, and a whole crowd of people will be there to surprise her. All the people who used to come to her restaurant and all the people who call her "Mama." And she'll hug every single one, the big people and the children, too.

And when I see that, when I see my grandma hugging people and making them happy, I'm going to forget all about that fly. Because then I'll know that some good *new* days are coming.

Yeah. For Grandma and me.